Mariella Mystery

Investigates

The HUge Hair Scare

Mariella Mystery

Investigates

The HUge Hair Scare

by
Kate
Pankhurst

BARRON'S

First edition for the United States published in 2014
by Barron's Educational Series, Inc.

First published in Great Britain in 2013 by Orion Children's Books,
a division of the Orion Publishing Group Ltd., Orion House,
5 Upper St. Martin's Lane, London WC2H 9EA, Great Britain

All inquiries should be addressed to:
Barron's Educational Series, Inc.
250 Wireless Boulevard, Hauppauge, New York 11788
www.barronseduc.com

ISBN: 978-1-4380-0461-7

Library of Congress Control No. 2014930541

Manufactured by B12V12G, Berryville, VA

Date of Manufacture: July 2014

Printed in the United States of America

9 8 7 6 5 4 3 2 1

For Dad and Andrew

me and my
totally ACE cat

THIS YOUNG SUPER SLEUTH JOURNAL BELONGS TO ...

MARIELLA MYSTERY: That's me. Talented Young Super Sleuth and Mystery Girl, aged nine and three quarters. Ready for any mystery. Especially a really scary or dramatic one.

This is my **top secret** journal. I'm trying to fine-tune my mystery senses by writing everything down, so everyone will think, "Wow, Mariella is a totally amazing detective."

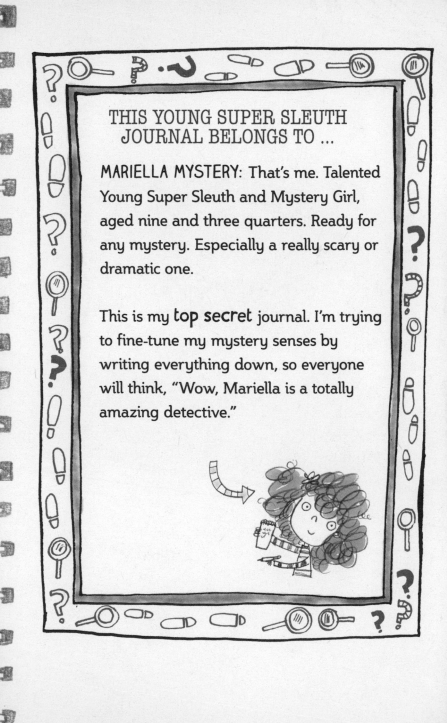

sniffer
dog

sniff

Suspicious
Finger print

Can't believe Mom won't let me have a sniffer dog! It's totally the most unfair thing ever. (And they aren't **THAT** hard to look after.)

mom

Sunday
October 25th

concentrating

picking up
a scent

ultra powerful nose

1:30 PM
GARDEN, 22 SYCAMORE AVENUE (MY HOUSE)

I have high hopes that Watson (pet cat and trusty sidekick) will become the world's first fully trained detective's sniffer cat.

SNIFFER CAT INTENSIVE TRAINING PROGRAM

NAME: WATSON MYSTERY

BREED: TOTALLY AMAZING SNIFFER CAT

doughnut

Watson

pizza

burger

fishy cat food

Watson's favorite foods

Expert Team of Cat Trainers (and Mystery Solvers)

Violet Maple

Mystery Girl and Chief Cat Behavior Analyst. Violet has been observing Watson's progress. She is totally allergic to cats so she has to do this from a safe distance (approximately five feet) to prevent sneezing fits.

Violet, blowing her nose

Poppy (being organized)

Poppy Holmes

Mystery Girl and Sniffer Cat Coaching Monitor. In charge of thinking up new challenges for Watson. She's really good at this because she is the team captain of our local synchronized swimming team, the Puddleford Puddles.

Mariella Mystery
(me)

Also a Mystery Girl and Chief Cat Handler. I know Watson best, so I've been guiding him through the intensive training challenges.

me ↶

KITTY CHALLENGE SIX: TRACKING THE SCENT OF A MISSING PERSON

10:00 AM: Poppy and I nominate Violet to be the missing person. Violet says she's not sure Watson is ready for this, but goes inside the house to hide.

10:07 AM: We let Watson sniff Violet's sweater and give him a clear instruction: "Find Violet, Watson, find Violet." (I read in the Young Super Sleuth's Handbook that it's important to give clear instructions to sniffer dogs. I'm sure the same is true for cats.)

Violet's sweater

10:10 AM: Watson heads toward the house and disappears through the cat flap. This is good. He is following Violet's scent!

cat flap

10:18 AM: Poppy and I go to investigate.

10:33 AM: We hear a screeching noise and thudding. Has Watson located Violet?

10:34 AM: Source of disturbing noise levels located in The Chief Cat Distractor's bedroom.

chief Cat Distractor

CHIEF CAT DISTRACTOR (AKA ARTHUR MYSTERY): Totally annoying little brother, aged five and three quarters.

10:35 AM: The true extent of Arthur's cat distraction is revealed. He's recently decided he wants to be just like his favorite pop star, Coco Nutello. The thudding noise was him dancing and the screeching was him singing. He has also recreated one of Coco Nutello's stupid hairstyles (a huge flip) on his hair and done the same to Watson.

Coco Nutello

FLIP

10:36 AM: Arthur says it's fine to put hairspray on a cat because it's Coco Nutello's own brand. (As if that makes a difference. You do not put hairspray on a cat!)

coco spray

stupid

10:37 AM: Mom comes in with Violet and demands to know what is going on. She found Violet trapped in the closet shouting for help. Whoops.

closet

HELP

10:38 AM: Training session is abandoned.

VERDICT: If Arthur hadn't behaved in such a distracting way, Watson would have tracked Violet down and raised the alarm that she was trapped. I'm not giving up. I'm sure Watson is destined to be the greatest sniffer cat, eventually.

trapped

sniff
sniff

TRAINING A SNIFFER DOG:

Have you ever wished you could follow the scent of a suspect or been frustrated that you can't identify the owner of some incriminating evidence? Sometimes we need a little help from our furry friends — Sniffer Dogs!

Train your sniffer dog to:

1. Follow the scent of a suspect or a missing person.

2. Perform a dancing routine to distract and confuse criminals so you can apprehend them.

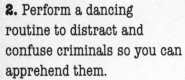

3. Help you with simple Mystery HQ-based tasks, like filing case reports and bringing you slippers to relax in.

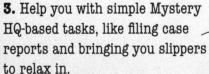

Discovering Famous Detectives: Sniffy McDuff

Sniffy McDuff shot to fame after he helped his owner, Trixie McDuff, to track a troop of prize-winning poodles. Sniffy saved the poodles from the terrible fate of being dyed pink and sold as Can-Can dancing circus dogs. He raised the alarm that the poodles were hidden in a cat grooming salon (the last place the dastardly dog-nappers thought anyone would look).

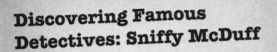

Sniffy – a handsome young Dachshund.

WARNING

Owning a sniffer dog is a big responsibility; in addition to hours of advanced training, your dog will need love, attention, and lots of exercise. Even sniffer dogs need a break from mystery solving.

WOOF! WOOF!

2:15 PM
22 SYCAMORE AVENUE (MY BEDROOM)

It's been really quiet since we solved our last big case, the Cupcake Conundrum. The Young Super Sleuth's Handbook says that a good detective never wastes time relaxing; he or she uses any non-mystery solving time to become a better detective. That's why this is the perfect opportunity to focus on things like Sniffer Cat Training.

me, being a better detective

I've been a little worried recently that nothing mysterious will ever happen again. But this is all part of being a detective – one day everything is completely normal, the next – BOOM! – a totally mysterious mystery arrives.

Poppy has gone now because she has to practice for the big swimming gala next week. She's determined the Puddleford Puddles will beat the Sunnyfield Swimmers. Poppy is really competitive with the team captain of the Sunnies, this stuck up girl called Pearl Swishay.

Pearl Swishay

Poppy

Violet went home quite soon after Poppy. I think she was a little upset about getting trapped in the closet. It's all Arthur's fault for being so obsessed with Coco Nutello.

Ever since Arthur heard Coco was coming to Puddleford on her Big Beautiful Hair Tour, he hasn't stopped talking about her. The Coco concert is this Saturday. Which is also Halloween – potentially the most mysterious day of the year.

coco nutello Presents

THE BIG Beautiful Hair TOUR

Halloween special!

frizz is for LOSERS!

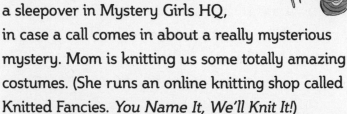

Poppy, Violet, and I are having
a sleepover in Mystery Girls HQ,
in case a call comes in about a really mysterious
mystery. Mom is knitting us some totally amazing
costumes. (She runs an online knitting shop called
Knitted Fancies. *You Name It, We'll Knit It!*)

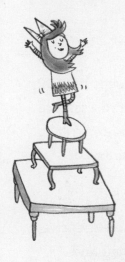

I don't see why Arthur is so
crazy about Coco. Her songs
are bad. The worst one is
all about dancing on tables.
She just sings the same line over
and over again. *I Love Dancin' on
Tables, Yeeeaahhhh!*

And as if anyone would go
around swishing their hair that
much – you'd just get weird looks if you did that
in real life.

The coco swish

2:45 PM
STILL IN MY BEDROOM

Arthur's CD

Arthur is being really annoying. He keeps begging Mom to take him to the fancy new hairdressers in Puddleford. It's called Hair by Marco – apparently Marco is a top celebrity stylist and used to do Coco Nutello's hair.

But Mom said Hair by Marco is far too expensive and Arthur will have to go to see Shirley and Barb at our usual hairdressers, Kurl Up and Dye* instead. Ha!

*KURL UP AND DYE: Usually people want to "curl up and die" (correct spelling) if they are embarrassed. Who wants to go to a hairdressers where you'll get embarrassing hair?

Last time Mom took us to Kurl Up and Dye, Barb spent two hours (which is a long time) blow drying my hair straight. I didn't even want straight hair and I lost valuable mystery solving time.

me with straight hair

A lot of the kids at school have gone crazy about Coco Nutello too. Miss Twist, our head teacher, is not very happy.

miss Twist (boring)

MISS TWIST: Head teacher of Puddleford Elementary School. Always in a mood about something. Currently on a mission to stop children from wearing any items that are not officially school uniform.

Miss Twist went crazy in assembly last week – she said if she sees students wearing Coco Nutello t-shirts under their school shirts, or with giant sequinned bows in their hair (Coco says big bows are "so in") they will be in BIG trouble.

BIG bow

She even told me to take off my detective's hat! Doesn't she realize I am doing a very serious and important job?

my hat

6:00 PM
MYSTERY GIRLS HQ

I've been preparing for the Astronomy Club
meeting tomorrow night. As well as training
Watson, Poppy, Violet, and I have also signed up
for Galaxy Gang. (That's what our Astronomy Club
is called.)

The poster in school said that we'd look for stars and
planets, but what I am really interested in is looking
for signs of alien activity. If the Mystery Girls spot a
UFO, we could solve the mystery of whether aliens
really do exist.

alien

Poppy and I have really gotten into it. The other day Poppy read about a man who said aliens sucked his brain out through his nostril then replaced it with an alien brain. Totally cool!

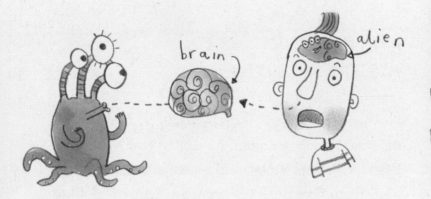

There have been some famous unsolved cases of extra-terrestrial* mysteries in the past, and if we look very carefully I'm sure we'll be able to discover whether aliens really are out there. Sebastian, who runs the Astronomy Club, thinks this is a great idea.

*EXTRA-TERRESTRIAL: Another way of saying that something is not from this planet (aliens).

SEBASTIAN: Runs Galaxy Gang and works at Puddleford Museum Planetarium.* Knows some totally-unbelievable-but-true facts about planets and asteroids. Also doesn't mind being called by his first name, which is cool, not like the teachers at school who get really mad about it.

Sebastian from Galaxy Gang

Violet says she's not sure there are such things as aliens. (I think this is because she'd be totally scared if she saw one.) But a good detective remains open-minded and doesn't get freaked out by aliens or closets.

*PLANETARIUM: Dark room with pictures of the solar system projected onto the ceiling. Makes you feel totally small compared to the size of Outer Space, which is BIG.

TYPES OF MYSTERY: EXTRA-TERRESTRIAL

This type of mystery is very rare, so rare that nobody is absolutely sure whether aliens do exist – but you should still be prepared for the possibility of alien activity. (A good Young Super Sleuth is prepared for anything.)

What To Expect In An Extra-Terrestrial Mystery:

1. Alien abduction of humans.

2. Sightings of unidentified flying objects (UFOs).

3. Distressed witnesses who claim to have seen an alien.

Little green men

Tall green men

Strange glowing blobs

Hoaxes: Things To Look Out For:

Alien costumes: If witnesses report seeing zips or buttons, the alien could actually be a human in disguise.

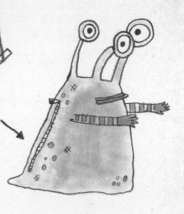

Alien footprints: Real or made by humans playing a practical joke?

Witness: Can you trust them? Could they be making up false alien sightings to scare others?

TOP TIP

Make sure you keep a camera with you at all times — you could be the first person ever to get conclusive evidence that aliens do exist!

alien LIFEFORMS→

Monday
October 26th

9:30 AM
BACK ROW, PUDDLEFORD ELEMENTARY
WHOLE SCHOOL ASSEMBLY

Something TOTALLY weird has just happened.

It started when Miss Twist barged into the hall halfway through a song Miss Crumble was playing on her guitar. (Miss Crumble is our totally ace class teacher. Her assemblies are always interesting, not like the boring ones Miss Twist does about being organized or not eating chips.)

miss Crumble

"This is completely unacceptable. Why can I STILL see children wearing glittery pumps and t-shirts with that stupid popstar's face on it, and those ridiculous giant bows?" she said.

I saw Jessie McDuff from the 4th grade trying to pull a giant shimmering Coco Nutello bow out of her hair.

huge

Bad move – Miss Twist spotted her right away. "YOU! Give me that now," she shouted.

As Miss Twist strode over to grab Jessie's bow, a bunch of kids started hiding their banned Coco Nutello items. I could see Arthur trying to help one of his annoying friends (I think her name is Pippa) by shoving her glittery beret under his shirt.

glittery beret

"You won't be getting any of this ridiculous stuff back for a LONG time," Miss Twist carried on. "And I expect all members of staff to be setting an example."

I looked around to where the teachers were sitting. Miss Twist was staring at Mr. Muffet (2nd grade teacher). He was wearing a woolly bobble hat. This didn't seem too bad, especially in comparison with those stupid bows.

"It's VERY important that I keep my hat on," said Mr. Muffet.

Mr. Muffet

bobble hat

"Mr. Muffet, I do not have time for this,"
Miss Twist said. "I insist that you remove that
bobble hat. NOW."

She gave Mr. Muffet one of her glares. They can
be totally scary – it's like they hypnotize you
or something. At the school bake sale last year,
I saw Miss Crumble pick up the last chocolate
cupcake. Miss Twist gave one of her looks and
Miss Crumble handed over the cake, just
like that.

SCARY
glare

cupcake

"Well, if that's what you want. Fine," said
Mr. Muffet. Then he pulled off his hat and the
whole hall gasped.

Mr. Muffet's hair is light brown and usually in a simple side parting style. But under his hat was a shockingly huge, tangled, bright pink, cotton candy nest. I couldn't believe it was actually his hair.

Miss Twist stared at Mr. Muffet, then she said, "Winners of the poetry competition, let's hear your poems. Hurry up!"

What? She goes completely crazy over headbands and hats, but doesn't say anything about a teacher with a huge wobbling pink new hairdo?

NEW MYSTERY TO SOLVE: WHAT is going on with Mr. Muffet's hair?

mr. Muffet's simple side parting

10:33 AM
SCHOOL PLAYGROUND, BREAK TIME

Mr. Muffet is on playground duty but it's impossible to get near to him. There are loads of giggling kids hanging around, probably hoping his bobble hat blows off so they get another glimpse of his crazy hair.

"I just don't get it. His hair is just so ... so ... pink!" said Poppy, covering her mouth so she didn't start laughing again. (She's been doing that all morning.)

"Maybe he had an accident with some hair dye?" said Violet.

hair dye

We don't know for sure and it's really hard to look for clues while he is still wearing his hat. This is what we've observed so far:

mr muffet

Wearing bobble hat again.

Stern face.
Doesn't look happy with new hair.

Arms folded.
Body language says I DO NOT want to speak to anyone.

Pink hair.
It's like it has a life of its own.

Touchy.
Keeps shouting at kids who go near him.

VERDICT: We need to get a closer look at Mr Muffet. Ask him some questions. We hope to locate him at lunchtime.

12:45 PM
SCHOOL LUNCH HALL

I'd suspected there was something weird going on
– but not this weird!

We discovered Mr. Muffet in the Chill Out Zone at
lunchtime. We deduced he must be hiding because
everyone kept laughing at him. We made sure
Poppy's giggling was under control and knocked on
the door.

At first there was silence, then Mr. Muffet said,
"Go away. I'm extremely busy."

But we weren't giving up that easily.
We went in anyway. Mr. Muffet was
sitting there, still wearing his bobble hat,
marking a pile of books.

"I suppose you've come to have a good laugh?" said Mr. Muffet.

"Actually, we came to see if you were OK," said Violet.

Mr. Muffet looked relieved, and a little surprised. (Good work, Violet.)

"That's very kind of you, girls," said Mr. Muffet. "I do feel rather silly."

Poppy nodded. We had said that she shouldn't speak if she thought she might laugh.

"We like your hair, it's ... different!" said Violet.

POPPY
trying not
to laugh.

"Different," Mr. Muffet said, staring into space. "That's one way to describe it."

"It looks totally cool! Did you decide to try a new look?" I said.

"NO I DID NOT! Look at me!" Mr. Muffet said. Then he totally lost it. **"Arrrgggghhh!"** he screamed, whipping off his bobble hat. The pink matted nest of hair sprung out. "I look like ...
I look like ... human cotton candy!"

Totally
WEIRD

I didn't know what to say. He was right.
Mr. Muffet's hair was even worse close up than it had been in the assembly.

"I don't understand how it happened," Mr. Muffet said.

"Mr. Muffet, you must have heard that we are really good at finding explanations for things," I said.

The Mystery Girls' work is well known at Puddleford Elementary. Miss Crumble was totally grateful when we helped her to figure out why there was a ghostly guinea pig in her backyard.

Mr. Muffet thought for a little while. Then he sighed.

"I suppose I can't look any sillier than I already do, I may as well tell you what happened ... but you'll never believe me," he said.

Ooooooh — MYSTERIOUS!

CASE REPORT
MR. MUFFET'S HAIR SCARE

7:40 PM: Mr. Muffet sets off home from Puddleford cinema. He's just watched Attack of the Zombie Aliens. (Poppy and I REALLY want to see this but Mom and Violet say it's way too scary. Nonsense!)

ZOMBIE alien

7:45 PM: Everything seems normal, until Mr. Muffet realizes he's walked into a thick patch of fog. He says the fog seemed to "appear from nowhere" and it was purple.

FOG

7:47 PM: The purple fog clears as suddenly as it arrived. Mr. Muffet thinks it was odd and he feels a little on edge after watching the scary movie so he walks a bit quicker.

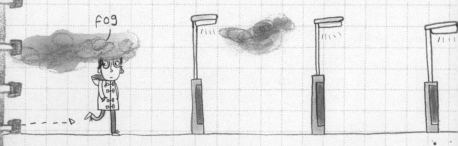

fog

8:00 PM: Arriving home, Mr. Muffet looks in the mirror — and screams. His hair is now a huge tangled, frizzy, pink mess. The only explanation Mr. Muffet can think of is that the weird purple fog caused his hair disaster.

8:22 PM: Washing it makes no difference. His hair is frozen in position and is still bright pink, so he wears an old bobble hat and hopes nobody will notice.

NEW MYSTERY TO SOLVE: Is there really a **Fog of Hair Horror*** floating around Puddleford?

<u>NOTES</u>: We suggested that Mr. Muffet visit his hairdresser to see if they can offer professional advice. Mr. Muffet said he's embarrassed to visit the hairdresser, or any other public place.

*Hair Horror: We are using this term to describe Mr. Muffet's hair, as it sounds really dramatic and catchy.

4:45 PM
MYSTERY GIRLS HQ

It's not every day you hear reports of **Fogs of Hair Horror**, so I decided to call a Mystery Girls team meeting before the Galaxy Gang meeting.

We won't be disturbed by Arthur being totally annoying like we usually are. He's at Kurl Up and Dye getting his Coco-Nutello-Concert-haircut. (Mom said it was really easy to get a last minute appointment there because Hair by Marco had stolen all their customers.)

annoying

Even though there is potentially a HUGE new mystery to solve, Poppy keeps going on about the swimming gala.

"Can you believe Pearl Swishay canceled her birthday party so she could practice?" Poppy said.

"Never mind Pearl Swishay. What about Mr. Muffet?" I said.

The Young Super Sleuth's Handbook says that a good detective always tries to find a logical explanation for strange events. This is what we came up with:

Logical Explanation One:

Mr. Muffet actually had a disaster with a home hair experiment and is so embarrassed, he is telling big fibs to cover it up. But would a teacher really make stuff up?

← towel

46

(Not Really) Logical Explanation Two:

Mr. Muffet fell victim to a weird weather phenomenon* causing strange effects on his hair. None of us had ever heard of a type of weather like this. (We know that drizzle makes your hair frizzy and if you were caught in a hurricane you might have quite tangled hair.)

(Very Unlikely) Logical Explanation Three:

Mr. Muffet encountered a fog cloud made by aliens, which produced his shocking new hairstyle. Sounds impossible but Mr. Muffet's hair is totally CRAZY.

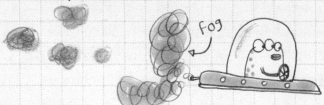

*PHENOMENON: Totally weird stuff, like a fog that turns your hair pink and freezes it into a crazy style.

47

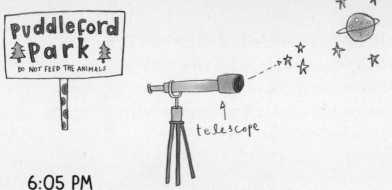

Puddleford Park ⤣Park⤣
DO NOT FEED THE ANIMALS

telescope

6:05 PM
PUDDLEFORD PARK, GALAXY GANG

The first thing we need to do is to look for more
clues that **The Fog of Hair Horror**
actually exists. Galaxy Gang tonight is the perfect
opportunity to look for aliens (as planned)
and any signs of a purple fog or people with bright
pink hair.

Violet said that we should only go outside if we
wear full head protection, especially since aliens
could have something to do with **The Fog**.
We're using these hats Mom knitted for us.

Tonight there is a full moon. Sebastian said it's a really good chance to observe its surface. He told us a totally cool fact: on Earth we can only ever see one side of the moon, because the other side is always facing away from us.

Interesting. The other side of the moon could be the perfect place for aliens to live undetected by humans. I know people have been to the moon before, but maybe the aliens all hid in the dark part so the astronauts didn't notice them? I'm sure if we just look really carefully, we'll see one.

comet

alien?

dark
side of
moon

6:25 PM
STILL AT PUDDLEFORD PARK

THE FOG HAS STRUCK AGAIN!!

I'd just seen a really big crater and was talking to
Sebastian about it, when I heard Violet scream and
Poppy shout,

"FOG! It's the fog!"

I looked up and it happened exactly like Mr. Muffet
said it did. Out of nowhere this weird purple fog
was swirling toward us. It was totally exciting and
confirmed we have a really weird case on our
hands! (Yay!)

"I can't see anything! MY HAIR

— what if it gets my hair?"

I heard Violet scream from nearby. (I need to
have a word with Violet later. Detectives need
to stay calm at all times.)

"Don't worry, dudes. Just a patch of fog, it'll clear
in a minute," called Sebastian. He was completely
chilled out, and probably wondering why Violet
was having such an extreme reaction. The other
members of Galaxy Gang didn't seem worried
either, but that's because none of them knew
what Mr. Muffet had told us.

I checked my own hair. Everything felt normal
under my hat. Then The Fog began to clear and
I could see shadowy figures.

Violet sprinted toward me. "I'm OK! The hat, it worked!" she said. "Are you OK, Mariella? Is Poppy?"

Before I could answer, someone staggered out of the fading Fog. I turned my flashlight onto Eloise Flack from 3rd grade and gasped.

Eloise's hair (which is normally in a neat blonde bob) was sticking up in wild spikes, as if she'd been struck by lightning. It was also a shocking bright green.

"What, what are you looking at me like that for?" said Eloise.

young super sleuth flashlight

arrrghh!

spikes

Eloise

I tried to remember what the Young Super Sleuth's Handbook said about breaking bad news to people gently, but couldn't find the right words to tell Eloise that she now looked like a mutant hedgehog.

mutant hedgehog

Eloise spotted Sebastian and the rest of the group. They all had the same electric shock hairstyle as she did. She gawked for a minute, then touched her own hair.

"Noooooo! What's going on?" she cried.

Then everyone was running around knocking over telescopes, shouting. But all I could think was – WOW! This mystery could be our most mysterious one yet!

THE HUGE HAIR SCARE: This is bigger than an isolated incident of Hair Horror; it has become one Huge Hair Scare.

6:40 PM
MOM'S CAR (TRAVELING BACK TO MYSTERY HQ)

When Mom came to pick up Poppy, Violet, and me, the parents were going crazy about the scary hair.

Mom was great. She volunteered to knit protective hats for everyone in Galaxy Gang. This seemed to reassure the parents – maybe because a hat would also conceal their children's hideously shocking hair.

Before Mom arrived, Poppy, Violet, and I managed to do a quick search of the area for clues. We've just done an in-car analysis of what we found:

EVIDENCE COLLECTED FROM PUDDLEFORD PARK (LAST KNOWN LOCATION OF THE FOG):

Empty chip bag, shrimp cocktail flavor — the favorite flavor chip of whoever is behind The Fog? (Do aliens eat shrimp cocktail chips?)

Size three glittery sneaker, left foot — probably lost in the panic of Hair Horror. May belong to a Coco Nutello fan.

empty

Large glass jar — is it a jam jar? (Do aliens eat jam?)

VERDICT: This looks like litter, but The Young Super Sleuth's Handbook says it's important to keep and catalog all pieces of evidence. They might seem irrelevant at the time but could later hold important clues.

Victims of Hair Horror: 13
(Galaxy Gang and Mr. Muffet)

7:15 PM
MYSTERY HQ, EMERGENCY MEETING

The Young Super Sleuth's Handbook says that after high drama situations it's important to stay focused and look at the facts. But the facts so far are mostly totally unbelievable – and totally exciting!

"I don't like this," Violet said. "Thirteen is a lot of victims, and a really unlucky number."

"Violet, we can't just abandon the case because it's getting scary," I said.

violet getting
stressed

"We've got to warn Puddleford then, tell everyone to wear a hat!" Violet said.

hats

She did have a point actually — we should have warned Galaxy Gang, but we weren't sure **The Fog** was real before tonight.

"We should issue some official Mystery Girl advice about how to avoid **The Fog**," I said.

"Yes," said Poppy. "What are we going to do if people are too scared to come and watch the swim meet on Wednesday?"

Honestly, the most exciting and mysterious case we've ever had and all Poppy is worried about is the swim meet!

7:40 PM
MYSTERY GIRLS HQ, BEANBAG AREA

We've looked at the facts and come up with a plan:

THE FOG: WHAT WE KNOW:

1. The Fog appears, as if from nowhere.

2. While in The Fog you can't see anything else.

3. The Fog has the power to transform hair into totally weird hairstyles in a short period of time.

4. The Fog is a little purple. (Unusual).

5. Hats protect hair from The Fog's effects.

SHOCKING EXAMPLES
of Hair Horror:

Electrified, stiff, windswept bright green hair.

Wild bird's nest, wispy, cotton candy-pink hair.

(Equally horrific, but different. Why is this?)

THEORIES ABOUT WHAT THE FOG IS:

A: Man-made. (But who would deliberately want to do that, and why?)

B: Not from this planet. (In other words alien!) Maybe aliens are experimenting on humans. If they are planning an invasion they might want us to look like them, so they feel more at home.

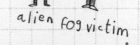

alien fog victim

<u>**VERDICT**</u>: Before we come to any conclusions we are going to speak to an expert on hair. We plan to visit Marco from Hair by Marco after school tomorrow. He does celebrities' hair so he must know loads of cool stuff.

The Fog has struck twice now; we need to warn the people of Puddleford they may be in danger by issuing Fog Avoidance Advice. (Dad's going to put it in the Puddleford Gazette for us — that's where he works.)

Galaxy Gang are deeply traumatized.

Hair Horror

Galaxy Gang members

shocking!

In total shock

Tuesday
October 27th

mr. Muffet brushing

Good news! Mr. Muffet just managed to brush one small section of hair. Interesting. Does this mean the effects of The Fog will fade over time?

12:45 PM
PLAYGROUND, LUNCHTIME

I can't believe Poppy. She took forever at the swim meeting, then came to tell us that Pearl Swishay and the Sunnyfield Swimmers have managed to get a day off school to practice for the swim meet. She didn't even ask how the Fog Avoidance Advice was going.

"The Sunnies are going to have an unfair advantage!" said Poppy. "I've told the Puddles to be prepared for some intensive swimming after school."

stupid
SWISHAY

After school? Wasn't she forgetting
something MAJORLY important?

"Poppy, we are going to
Hair by Marco after
school, remember?"

*totally
unfocused*

"You two will be fine
without me. And once
I've won this meet I'll
be back on the case!" she
said. "Got to go – we are
doing some leg stretches to get
ready. Call you later."

Then she just went off, like there isn't a **Fog of
Hair Horror** floating around at all.

Unbelievable!

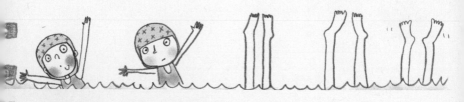

Violet is worried we won't be able to handle any sudden reports of Fog Attacks without Poppy, but I'm sure we'll cope. You never know, we might make a breakthrough with the case and then I'll be far too busy to speak to Poppy when she calls.

Fog Victims: 14
(The Fog has struck again!)

4:03 PM
OUTSIDE HAIR BY MARCO, PUDDLEFORD MAIN STREET

This salon is totally chic. I haven't seen any of Marco's haircuts yet, but I'm impressed by the trees outside shaped like heads (with nice haircuts).

fancy trees

We are trying to work out how to deal with a situation. There's a girl sitting behind the reception desk with totally crazy hair. It's another Fog Victim!

This means that The Fog has struck three times now. Why didn't we know about this one?

The Fog Victim looks as if she's in a terrible mood.
Her hair really is hideous. Black with pink tips,
spiked in all different directions.

Fog Victim!

It is probably a good thing that Poppy didn't
come with us. This woman does not look like
she would put up with any laughing.

"We need to tread carefully, Violet," I said.
"She could have vital clues about The Fog."

"I don't like this, Mariella," said Violet. "If a girl working at a hairdresser's can't fix her own Fog Hair, maybe that means there's no cure for it. I can't bear to think of Mr. Muffet and Galaxy Gang stuck with **Hair Horror** forever!"

Violet was being a little dramatic, but she's right. This is a totally amazing mystery, except it's not amazing that Mr. Muffet and everyone from Galaxy Gang are being laughed at everywhere they go.

We're going in.

fog victims

ha ha ha!

Fog Victims: 13 (not 14 as previously reported)

4:10 PM
INSIDE HAIR BY MARCO, WAITING FOR MARCO

The receptionist didn't look up as we came in. She just kept reading her magazine. On the walls of the salon there are a lot of pictures of celebrities striking a pose with a man who has a jet black flip and a beard. I have deduced this must be Marco.

Rara La Floop

Janey-Jane

smooth Boyz

Bertie-B

Cherry Lips

The biggest picture is one of Coco Nutello hugging Marco. No wonder Arthur is desperate to meet him – from the picture it looks like Marco and Coco are best friends.

coco nutello

"Name?" the girl at reception said, still not looking up.

"Um, well, I'm Mariella, and this is Violet." I said. "We'd like to see Marco, please."

"Do you have an appointment? Marco is very busy doing a Style Innovation," she said. "He can't see you unless you have an appointment."

I said that it was urgent, that we were investigating The Fog, trying to help **Hair Horror** victims.

"You what?" she said.

Violet and I looked at each other. We thought she must be in denial after her scary ordeal with **The Fog**.

"I can't help noticing that you might need our help too. Your hair is ... it's quite unusual, isn't it?" I said.

"Yeah, what's your point?" said the receptionist. "I like to experiment, be a little different. That's what we do at Hair by Marco. No boring styles here."

THE Salon

hair

"So, um, you aren't a Fog Victim then?" I said. I couldn't believe that anyone would actually choose to have hair in such a weird style.

"Listen, I don't know what point you are trying to make but if you haven't got an appointment, you can't see Marco. He's far too busy."

"It won't take long, we'll just wait here until Marco's free," Violet said politely, sitting down in the waiting area next to a lady we thought must be Marco's next customer.

I hope we don't have to wait much longer, I'm trying to look really interested in a magazine about hair. (It's totally dull.)

HAIR FACT: I've just read that the "messed up" look is really "in" this season. That might cheer the Fog Victims up a bit.

4:25 PM
OUTSIDE STUFFED (CAKE SHOP)

Our conversation with Marco didn't go exactly according to plan.

When Marco appeared, he was with a customer. She had crazy hair, not Fog-Hair-crazy, but it was cut shorter on one side than on the other and her bangs were at a weird angle.

crazy

BIG flip

Marco

"Which one of you is my next client?" Marco said, staring at us and the lady who was waiting.

He didn't smile or anything, which was a little unfriendly, but I thought maybe he just took Style Innovations very seriously.

"Those girls don't have an appointment, Marco. I told them they have to leave but they won't go," said the receptionist.

"Marlene! I cannot work with such disorganization," said Marco. "And WHERE is my cappuccino?"

a cappuccino

I decide to take decisive action.

comb

"Actually we wanted to ask you some
questions. We've heard you know
absolutely everything about hair,
and we love your work with Coco Nutello,"
I said. (The Young Super Sleuth's Handbook says
that flattering somebody is a great way to get them
on your side.)

"Yes, well. Coco and I go way back. I created her
famous hair swish, you know," Marco said.

"This may sound unbelievable, but we have
information that suggests a large – possibly
alien – fog is floating around Puddleford, causing
some strange effects on hair," I said.

Marco just looked at us. I thought we'd better show
him some actual evidence to back up our story.

"There have been thirteen Fog
Victims that we know about so far,"
I said, holding up the photos of
Mr. Muffet and the Galaxy Gang.

fog victim

yawn

But Marco didn't seem even a little shocked. In fact, he looked bored.

This was not what I'd been expecting at all.

I carried on anyway. "We wondered if you've got some advice for Fog Victims?" I said.

Marco sighed, as if he couldn't be bothered to answer us. "Stay indoors. Nobody wants to see bad hair. Certainly don't come here – I can't have the place cluttered up with these so called 'Fog Victims.' It'll upset my regular customers."

Unbelievable!

How could a hairdresser not want to help these people?

rollers

We can't just tell Fog Victims there's no hope of normal hair. We need to speak to another, more helpful hair expert. I'm not totally sure they are hair experts, but we are going to go to Kurl Up and Dye. It's worth a try.

Barb

Can they help?

Shirley

Arthur's concert flip haircut styled at Kurl Up and Dye. Hmmmm.

Huge

5:15 PM
OUTSIDE KURL UP AND DYE

When we arrived the salon was empty. (Mom was
right about them having no customers.)

On the walls, there were some really ancient-looking
photos of models with old-fashioned hairstyles.
I didn't think there was much chance Shirley
and Barbara had ever styled a celebrity's hair.
But judging by the pictures, they
had been hairdressers for a long
time, so maybe they would know
something useful.

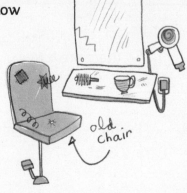

old chair

Shirley walked out from the back of the shop carrying two cups of tea.

"BARBARA," she shouted. "Customers!"

Barb was fast asleep under this old-fashioned hairdryer hood thing. We'd just walked right past her.

Barb asleep

hair'o'matic

"Mariella, isn't it? And Violet! What can we do for you?" said Shirley.

I explained about the **Fog of Hair Horror** and showed them photographs of the victims.

"So there are a few of these victims? Isn't that awful, Barb?" said Shirley.

"I've never seen anything like it, Shirl," said Barbara.

"Do you think you'd be able to do anything for the victims?" I said.

worried about HAIR HORROR

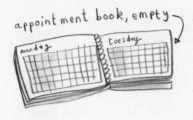
appointment book, empty

"We'll certainly do our best. I can make some appointments now, if you'd like?" said Shirley. "When is good for you? Any time is good for us."

"We could try that high strength shampoo that's been in the back for years," said Barbara.

They were totally great. Not like Marco. I'm really hoping their high strength shampoo works. At the moment, Barb and Shirley are the best the Fog Victims can hope for.

High strength shampoo

6:00 PM
MY HOUSE, KITCHEN (22 SYCAMORE AVENUE)

We've just got back. Mom has finished the hats for the Galaxy Gang and Mr. Muffet. They aren't just any old hats – they are knitted hairstyle hats!

She's made one for Arthur in the shape of his new flip.

"My new hairstyle is protected from The Fog! Nothing will happen to it before the Coco concert!" he beamed.

hairstyle hat ➡

He's such a wimp. I bet he begged Mom to knit him that hat when she was already totally busy knitting hats for real Fog Victims.

"Let's just hope the aliens haven't started abducting people by then. It would be a terrible shame if you went missing," I said.

alien abducting ARTHUR

Arthur looked worried. "What do you mean?"

"Just a suspicion we're working on. It seems highly likely that The Fog is the work of aliens," I said.

"You're making it up!" said Arthur.

"If you say so," I said. "Go away. Violet and I have important mystery solving work to do."

Actually, Dad needs the Fog Avoidance Advice by 7 pm. That's less than an hour.

Arrrggghhh!

8:23 PM
MY HOUSE, KITCHEN TABLE

TERRIBLE NEWS!

Poppy's mom has just called to tell us that Poppy and her entire synchronized swimming team have been caught in a **Fog Attack**.

Mom took the message because we were in Mystery Girls HQ finishing our Fog Avoidance Advice. (I keep saying I need a working phone line in there, for emergencies like this!)

As usual, Mom didn't ask any of the right questions. We can only assume it must be bad if Poppy hasn't been able to call herself.

We've been trying to call Poppy's house, but there's no answer. Violet is panicking about alien involvement, but I said we need to remain calm and we also need to question Poppy. Maybe she saw where The Fog came from. (If it was an alien, I hope she was carrying her Young Super Sleuth camera.)

There's probably no chance of the Puddles winning the meet now. Not if the entire team have Fog Hair. Pearl Swishay and the Sunnies will take home the trophy and Poppy will never live it down. I feel a little bad for getting annoyed with her.

9:30 PM
MY BEDROOM, MYSTERY DESK

HANG ON! What if we've been missing
something all along ...? PEARL SWISHAY!

What if it's Pearl and
not aliens like we
thought? Is she so
desperate for her
team to win that she
created a **Fog of
Hair Horror**?

SUSPECT?

Mom said it's too late to try calling Poppy again
now, but I know if I could just ask her what she
saw, there might be a clue to tell us who is behind
The Fog.

10:25 PM
MY BEDROOM, IN BED

I've made a map of all the locations The Fog has caused Hair Horror so far and it has revealed an important clue – all of them have happened very near to Puddleford Main Street! I have called these **Hair Horror Hotspots**.

Is Pearl releasing The Fog after she's been swimming? (Her team practices at Puddleford Pool too.) But why would she target Mr. Muffet?

Or if it's aliens (we can't rule them out just yet), why would they be targeting the Main Street?

Wednesday
October 28th

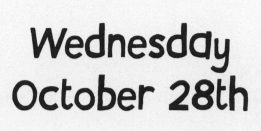

8:00 AM
MY KITCHEN, AGAIN (22 SYCAMORE AVENUE)

Still no one answering the phone at Poppy's house. Violet and I are going to call around on the way to school.

I showed Violet the map I'd made and told her my theory. She hadn't even thought Pearl Swishay could be behind the whole thing. She was too worried about Poppy and aliens.

But there's some good news – our Fog Avoidance Advice has gone in the Gazette! Wow, it makes us sound really professional. Hopefully this will prevent more **Fog Victims**. (I just wish Poppy had read this before last night.)

Fog Avoidance Advice

issued by the Mystery girls

WARNING! MYSTERIOUS FOG HITS PUDDLEFORD

This Fog produces some very unusual side effects on hair. The Mystery Girls are currently investigating where it is coming from and what to do about it.

We do not wish to alarm anyone, but due to the extreme effects on human hair we haven't ruled out that this fog could be extra-terrestrial.

Victim of Hair Horror

AVOIDING FOG HAIR:

1. If you see a **swirling purple fog**, run as fast as you can in the opposite direction.

2. Wear a hat at all times — you can get really cool ones from Knitted Fancies that look just like your normal hair.

3. Be vigilant* at all times. We don't know when, or if, The Fog may strike again.

***Vigilant:** Noticing everything around you, like a Fog of Hair Horror.

WHAT SHOULD I DO IF I HAVE FOG HAIR?

1. Don't panic. The effects of The Fog will fade gradually. (We are unsure if they will disappear completely.)

2. Make the most of your new look! Wear a sweater that matches your hair color.

3. Seek professional advice. The stylists at Kurl Up and Dye (17 Main Street) have said they will try to resolve any Fog-related hair issues to the best of their abilities.

4. Contact the Mystery Girls. We are logging all incidents of Hair Horror and promise not to laugh at your strange hair. (Mystery Girls, 22 Sycamore Avenue, Puddleford.)

curtains closed

8:35 AM
17 NUTBUSH AVENUE, POPPY'S BEDROOM
(POPPY'S HOUSE)

We pushed Poppy's bedroom door open.
The curtains were closed. I could just make
out that Poppy was in bed, the
covers over her face.

I had a sudden thought.
What if Poppy wasn't Poppy
anymore and she was just a
big ball of hair? Then a muffled
voice said, "Don't look at me!"

help

hair

"Poppy! We thought you'd been abducted by
aliens!" said Violet. (Actually it was just Violet
who'd thought that.)

"Come on! It can't be that bad," I said, opening the curtains.

The light streamed through the window and I got a good look at the top of Poppy's head. Her hair looked completely normal. What?

"Poppy! Your hair is fine. What's going on?" I said. Violet and I had been worried all night, so if there wasn't something really dramatic going on, I was going to be totally annoyed.

She lifted her head and we saw what the problem was. Where Poppy's eyebrows should have been were two fuzzy, frizzy balls of white hair.

CASE REPORT
POPPY HOLMES'S HAIR SCARE

7:00 PM: After a practice session at Puddleford Pool, Poppy and the rest of the team go for a jog.

7:10 PM: Poppy puts on her swimming cap and tells everyone else to wear theirs too, but they refuse, thinking they will look silly.

swimming cap

7:12 PM: While jogging, Poppy catches a glimpse of a large shadow moving near an alleyway up ahead. Sensing danger, Poppy shouts for everyone to turn around.

7:13 PM The team are running in synchronized formation, and nobody is sure who is supposed to lead. So they keep running — straight into The Fog Cloud flowing out of the alleyway.

shadow

fog ↑

7:15 PM: Poppy can't see any of her team through the thick purple swirl. All she can hear is a weird whirring noise. (An alien spacecraft?)

7:18 PM: The Fog clears and the swimmers realize, to their horror, that they all have cotton wool for hair.

cotton wool hair

7:19 PM: Poppy thinks she is safe because she's wearing her swimming cap, so she runs to the alleyway to see if she can figure out where The Fog came from. She doesn't see anything strange.

7:22 PM: Back in the pool changing rooms, Poppy looks in the mirror. Catching a glimpse of her Fog Brows for the first time, she is horrified.

7:25 PM: Poppy forgets all her Mystery Girl training and runs home to hide in her bedroom. She's too upset to call me or Violet, and feels really guilty for laughing at Mr. Muffet.

Fog Brows

2:00 PM
WHOLE SCHOOL TRIP TO PUDDLEFORD POOL, AUDIENCE SEATING AREA

The swim meet was a BAD IDEA. The Puddles were determined to not let the Fog Hair stop them from winning, especially when they found out Pearl was under suspicion, but it was pretty awful to watch.

When they came out from the locker rooms the audience couldn't stop laughing. Pearl Swishay and her team looked totally delighted, whispering to each other and giggling.

swimming hat

"If it was Pearl, she's not even feeling the least bit guilty," said Violet.

She was right. But does that mean she is behind all this Hair Horror? I'm just not sure how she could have made a Fog so powerful. She's only nine. Is she just really good at science?

evil science genius

The Fog Hair weighed the team down, making it impossible for them to swim in formation. Poppy tried her best, but her Fog Brows were hanging in front of her eyes so she could hardly see at all.

The Sunnyfield Swimmers won. They completed their routine perfectly while the Puddles had to sit and watch.
Poppy looked totally devastated.

wet fog brows

4:00 PM
KURL UP AND DYE, FOG BROW TREATMENT IN PROGRESS

There has been good news, bad news, and more good news ...

GOOD NEWS: EXTRA STRENGTH SHAMPOO IS WORKING:

Poppy's treatment is almost done and her eyebrows are still weird but less frizzy. Shirley and Barbara said because Poppy is a Mystery Girl, she doesn't have to pay for her treatment. Nice!

less frizzy

BAD NEWS: NO MORE GALAXY GANG:

Sebastian has just been into Kurl Up and Dye to book a De-Foggifying Treatment. He told us Miss Twist is really angry about the Galaxy Gang's hair and has canceled the club. Totally unfair!

spikes drooping

sebastian

MORE GOOD NEWS: SEBASTIAN CAN ANALYZE THE FOG:

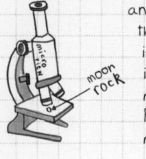

moon rock

I didn't think about it before, but Sebastian is a scientist and he analyzes pieces of moon rock at the museum all day. He said if we can get a sample of it he might be able to reveal more clues about what The Fog is, and who might have made it. (Aliens, or Pearl?)

The Mystery Girls will be out there tonight, trying to get a Fog sample for Sebastian!

Fog Victims: 25
(Whoops)

6:00 PM
MY HOUSE, KITCHEN (22 SYCAMORE AVENUE)

We've just returned from Operation Fog Grab. Here is my mission report in full:

OPERATION FOG GRAB

THE PLAN: Track The Fog using Watson's amazing sense of smell, then obtain a sample for scientific testing. (To be performed by temporary, definitely for one night only, Mystery Girl, Arthur Mystery.)

Watson   me   Violet   Poppy   Arthur

4:30 PM: I persuade Mom there could be more Fog Victims if we don't stick Fog Avoidance Advice up in town. (This is sort of true - we'll do that after we've got a Fog Sample.)

4:40 PM: I tell Violet to stop asking if everyone has their hats pulled over their eyebrows. She could be drawing unwanted attention to us.

4:45 PM: We arrive at Main Street and get Watson to sniff Poppy's eyebrows. (We hope they might still smell like The Fog.)

smells like FOG?

4:55 PM: We follow Watson to the alley at the side of Stuffed (cake shop). Are we about to find out where The Fog is coming from?

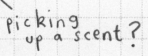

picking up a scent?

4:57 PM: I tell Arthur this is his chance to be a Mystery Girl. All he needs to do is to fill an empty peanut butter jar with Fog if he sees any. He has Watson for support.

4:58 PM: Arthur goes down the alley. Everything is quiet. Then he shouts that Watson has found some cake on the floor. False alarm. No Fog.

4:59 PM: Suddenly we hear a strange whirring noise. Is this the same whirring noise Poppy heard just before her Fog Attack?

5:00 PM: There is a high-pitched scream. Arthur! Then we see it. At the other end of the alleyway, The Fog is coming toward us.

5:01 PM: Now there is a loud crashing in the Fog-filled alleyway. Could it be Pearl? Or an alien?

5:04 PM: The Fog fades. The Mystery Girls are unharmed. Arthur appears from the alleyway. His hairstyle hat is hanging off one side of his head, and on the other side is a matted purple wobbling beehive of Fog Hair. Watson is with Arthur — he has Fog Fur! He is all matted and has a weird little beehive.

Beehive

Fog Fur!

5:05 PM: Arthur holds up the peanut butter jar. It's filled with swirling Fog. We have our sample! Success!

OUTCOME: <u>MISSION SUCCESSFUL.</u>
(Apart from Arthur's Fog Hair and Watson's Fog Fur.)

Thursday October 29th

FOG!

peanut butter

THE SAMPLE

violet
(being nervous)

8:40 AM
PUDDLEFORD MUSEUM

We've just dropped off The Fog sample with Sebastian. He said his test would prove whether or not The Fog is from this planet. If Pearl made it there might be traces of swimming pool (because she spends so much time in there). We could be about to get our biggest clue yet about who is behind The Fog!

alien   Pearl

Violet is worrying as usual. "I can't help feeling bad about Arthur's hair," she said.

"At least now he knows being a Mystery Girl is tough work," I said. "And anyway, Mom's persuaded him Coco will love it."

Mom and Dad said it was irresponsible of us to send Arthur into The Fog Cloud, especially when I'd said we were only going to stick up Fog Avoidance Advice. I don't know what all the fuss is about – it's only one side of his head that is affected. All I can think about is how I can't wait a whole day for news about the Fog sample.

Arggghhhh!

3:45 PM
PUDDLEFORD MUSEUM

The results are back and they aren't what I was
expecting at all – this is what Sebastian found in
the Fog sample:

FOG OF HAIR HORROR REPORT:

Hairspray (very concentrated)

Dry Shampoo

clean scalp

Hair wax

wax

hair dye

Pink and purple hair-dye

Teabags

glue

Perming lotion (high strength)

Weird. How would aliens get hold of all this hairdressing stuff? It looks likely that the Fog is the work of somebody who lives on this planet. But who?

We aren't totally sure it could have been Pearl now either. Surely she can't be *that* good at science. Whoever made The Fog is very intelligent. They managed to create different formulations for Fog so it transforms hair into the shocking styles we've seen. There wasn't anything swimming-related in it either.

The Mystery Girls have some serious work to do. This case feels like it is in serious danger of remaining **UNSOLVED**.

(Disaster!)

**4:45 PM
MYSTERY GIRLS HQ**

We have new suspects! The Young Super Sleuth's Handbook is right – if you can't figure out what a clue means, you need to look closer at the evidence. We thought about this for a while, and then I realized we'd been so focused on aliens and Pearl that we'd missed something obvious.

"This is someone who knows what those products can do," I said. "Could it be the work of a professional hairdresser?"

"That's crazy! Why would a hairdresser want to make people look hideous?" said Poppy.

"I don't know. But who else would know how to do such weird things to hair?" I said.

"Mariella, are you saying it's one of the hairdressers in Puddleford?" Violet said, shocked. "I mean, Marco was horrible, but he REALLY hates bad hair."

"And it can't be Barb and Shirley at Kurl Up and Dye," said Poppy. "They've been so helpful and nice about my Fog Brows."

Nothing is adding up. Violet said we should write a list of suspects and motives. It might help with our logical thinking.

straightener

hair

hair

Suspect FACTS

The Fog is mostly made up of hairstyling products that were expertly mixed to cause maximum **Hair Horror**. You need to know stuff about hair to do this.

galaxy gang

mr. muffet

Puddle

SUSPECT ONE: Kurl Up and Dye. Run by (the very helpful) Shirley and Barbara.

MOTIVE: Their salon has been really quiet since Hair by Marco opened. Did they create The Fog to get more customers? Is that how they knew how to cure it? They were very eager to fit people in. Too eager?

SUSPECT TWO: Hair by Marco. Could it have been unfriendly celeb hairdresser Marco and his moody assistant, Marlene?

MOTIVE: We aren't sure. WHY would Marco do this when he is only interested in creating Hair Innovations? He could have wanted to create bad hair days to get more customers, but if that was true, why would he refuse to treat Fog victims? Marlene has crazy hair, but she denies it is Fog Hair. Is this true?

VERDICT: We need more evidence. Poppy says she really hopes it isn't Shirley and Barbara because they are just so nice. Violet has a bad feeling about Marco but that doesn't mean he did it. (This case is totally the most difficult one ever!)

MYSTERY SENSES: SUSPICIONS

Your Young Super Sleuth's Mystery Senses may be telling you there is something suspicious about a person, even though there is no concrete evidence to prove it. Don't get carried away. Before taking drastic action, like making an accusation, check how tuned in your Mystery Senses actually are.

A Hunch

A person is acting strangely but you aren't sure if this is related to the case. Don't do anything right away, just add them to your list of **potential suspects** and keep watching.

A Funny Feeling

Something isn't quite right but you can't put your finger on what that is – remain **open-minded**. Maybe you are a little tired, or have eaten something that didn't agree with you.

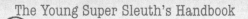

A Strong Suspicion

You can think of a possible **motive** to suggest a person is involved with a mystery. Without evidence, this is just a theory. Organize a **surveillance trip** to identify concrete evidence this person is definitely involved.

Something Fishy

(Not literally) You suspect somebody isn't telling the truth. Look for physical evidence of fibbing. Is the person fidgeting, or sweating?

Absolute Certainty

Your Mystery Senses are backed up with some **concrete evidence**. When you have a suspicion AND evidence you can make an accusation or apprehend somebody.

WARNING

Don't be fooled. Watch out for extra sneaky suspects who are trying to trick your Mystery Senses by being extra nice or appearing shocked by a terrible incident. (It's probably best to Trust Nobody.)

6:00 PM
MYSTERY GIRLS HQ

Tomorrow after school we are going undercover to try and catch one of our suspects doing something highly incriminating (like releasing The Fog).

We've got the perfect disguises –
Mom finished our Halloween
sleepover costumes.
(They have built-in
eyebrow protectors!)

Arthur's just come in. He wanted to show us what Barb and Shirley at Kurl Up and Dye have done to his half-beehive. It still looks weird, but now it's a little less purple. He also had news he thought we'd be dying to hear about Coco Nutello.

floppy

"She's still coming! Coco said she can't desert Puddleford – not when they need her Beautiful Big Hair Tour to keep their spirits up!" he shouted.

"Go away! We do not have time to talk about the stupid Coco Nutello concert," I said.

Violet said, "Mariella, I don't like this."

STUPID!

I thought Violet was just nervous about the surveillance mission, but then she said, "I'm talking about the Coco Nutello concert. The whole town is going to be there. What if there is a Fog Attack? All of Puddleford could end up with Fog Hair!"

Distraught

"What if something happens to Coco? Nooooooo!" said Arthur.

"Don't panic," I said. I hadn't thought of that. "There is nothing to suggest the Coco concert is a target. And if it is, well, we'll just have to solve the mystery before then."

Oh no. What do we do if all of Puddleford gets Fog Hair?

5:15 PM
OUTSIDE KURL UP AND DYE

Poppy, Violet, and I are
lying low behind the
sandwich board
advertising "Help for Fog
Victims Here." Nobody
will find us. (If they do
they might just think
it's weird seeing three
knitted aliens.)

lying LOW →

Through the window we can
see Shirley tapping numbers
into a calculator. Could this
have something to do with
the formula for The Fog?

$x/y \div z = fog$!

Barbara is heading toward the back of the salon. She's grabbed a cookie, and is now sitting under one of the old-fashioned hairdryer hoods.

"Do you think those weird hairdryers could have anything to do with The Fog?" said Violet.

Fog maker?

"It just seems to be drying Barb's hair at the moment," I said. "But who knows what they use it for when the shop closes."

The salon closes in fifteen minutes. Shirley and Barbara don't seem to be in any sort of rush to close up. Is that because they are waiting around to continue their campaign of **Hair Horror?**

5:40 PM
STILL OUTSIDE KURL UP AND DYE

We just overheard Shirley and Barbara talking as they closed the shop and they weren't hatching an evil plan to go out and ruin people's hair.

"It's a terrible to-do, this Fog," said Barbara.

"I know, Barb, but good to be busy again!" said Shirley. "There isn't much of that extra-strong shampoo left. We might need to start asking for donations if we're going to be able to get some more in. The till is pretty empty."

empty

"Like a charity? Help the Victims of Hair Horror?" said Barbara.

"Good idea! Let's ask those nice mysterious girls to help us," said Shirley.

HELP THE
Victims of
HAIR
HORROR

We all looked at each other.

"So it wasn't only me who got a free treatment!" said Poppy. "They just want to help the victims."

"Hang on. What if they knew we were watching them? It could be a cover up," I said.

We're going over to Hair by Marco now. Hopefully they haven't gone home yet – we have some more investigating to do!

sneaky?

5:50 PM
BEHIND THE GARBAGE CANS OUTSIDE
OF HAIR BY MARCO

Marlene – the receptionist – looks even more crazy today than she did on Tuesday. I almost didn't recognize her. She hasn't got black hair anymore. Now it's all piled up on top of her head in a bumpy purple and white frizzy beehive.

WEIRD ALERT!

122

I've seen that style before!
I grabbed the photo of Arthur's
Fog Hair out of my pocket and
showed it to Poppy and Violet.

Arthur's beehive

"Her hair, it looks like Arthur's
Fog Hair!" said Poppy.

"What if Marlene is the one making The Fog?"
I said. "She wants everyone to look as strange
as she does!"

"What about Marco?
Do you think he's in on
it too? His hair looks
normal," said Violet.

normal

This is all highly
suspicious. And it's now
been twenty minutes
since the salon closed.
Why are they both hanging around? They have
disappeared into the back of the shop now. We
can't see a thing.

**5:55 PM
STILL BEHIND THE GARBAGE CANS
OUTSIDE HAIR BY MARCO**

POTENTIAL INCRIMINATING EVIDENCE DISCOVERED!

While Marco and Marlene were in the back of the salon we decided to search the garbage cans. (The Young Super Sleuth's Handbook says this is a good way of finding clues that suspects think have been disposed of.)

We found a few things – empty shampoo bottles, magazines – but there was something else that could be relevant.

It's a glass jam jar, identical to the one we found at the scene of the Galaxy Gang Fog Attack. Is this the evidence we have been looking for? Can we link them to the scene of the Galaxy Gang Fog Attack? Or have they just been eating jam at Hair by Marco?

magazine

?

magazine

style amazing HAIR

Hair for you

cup

clip

hair

teabag

Sandwich (cheese and pickle)

shampoo   shampoo

empty shampoo bottles

6:05 PM
STILL OUTSIDE HAIR BY MARCO
(NOW AROUND THE BACK)

DEFINITE SUSPICIOUS ACTIVITY ALERT!

We decided to come around the back of the salon to see if we could figure out what Marco and Marlene were up to.

There was a light on in the back window. It was risky, but a good detective sometimes needs to take risks, so I crept to the window and found myself looking into some kind of staff room.

Marco was standing with his back to me. There was no sign of Marlene. He seemed to be talking, even though there was nobody else there. He was waving his hands about as if he was angry. Weird.

waving arms

my view through the window

Then Marco started clutching at his hair. He waved his hands around, and suddenly he knocked something off his head.

It took me a second to realize that the thing Marco had knocked off his head was a wig! He has no hair!

wig!

Marco bent to pick up the wig and I saw a picture pinned to the wall in front of him. I grabbed my Young Super Sleuth binoculars to get a closer look. It was the photo of him and Coco Nutello.

I don't get it. Why is he shouting at a picture of Coco Nutello, who he's meant to be really good friends with? What is going on?

Coco and Marco

coco nutello

8:20 PM
MY BEDROOM, 22 SYCAMORE AVENUE

MAJOR BREAKTHROUGH ALERT!!

I decided to do some research on Coco and
Marco after what we'd just witnessed. And I've
just discovered something totally shocking on
the Official Coco Nutello Fansite. I've printed it to
show Poppy and Violet.

me, confused

Exclusive!

Official Big Beautiful Hair Interview

Good news, Nutello Nuts! Coco's taken time out of her very busy schedule to tell us about her brand new Big Beautiful Hair products and a little about where she finds inspiration for her unique style.

Coco, your hair is fab. How did you achieve the look?

It looks great, doesn't it? I take my personal hair stylist wherever I go. I'm so busy, I don't have time to blow dry my own hair. It's, like, sooooo hard being me!

BUY NOW
BIG BOWS

You aren't afraid to try out some radical new looks. Where do you get your ideas from?

My new hairdresser is completely inspirational. He showed me a picture of this poodle and I was, like, "YEAH! Make me look like that." I've had some bad hairdressers though — I had to fire one for being bald. Can you imagine, me, with a BALD hairdresser? Embarrassing!

Your hair care range is proving really popular – we hear there are some brand new products about to be released.

Wohooh! I'm so excited about that. We've got this new spray that makes it really easy to flick your hair about. Like this.

Love 'n' Hugs to all my Nutello Nuts!

Oh, wow. We know Marco used to be Coco's hairdresser and now I've discovered he is bald and angry at her. Could Marco be the bald hairdresser that Coco fired?

What does this mean?

Aaarrrrrggggh! I need to talk to Poppy and Violet!

9:00 AM
MYSTERY GIRLS HQ

"I don't like this at all," said Violet. "Coco is coming to Puddleford TOMORROW! If Marco wants revenge, it's the perfect opportunity."

It didn't make sense last night, but if Marco is the hairdresser Coco fired, he now has a motive for creating Fog Hair – revenge! Violet and Poppy were amazed when I showed them the interview.

We still don't know for sure whether Marco is the bald hairdresser fired by Coco, or if he is the one behind The Fog. But, out of all our suspects, he seems to be the most suspicious.

SUSPICIOUS THINGS ABOUT MARCO (AND MARLENE)

1. There is a high concentration of hairdressing products in The Fog. Marco and Marlene have access to all these products. (But so do Shirley and Barb.)

2. Marlene's hair looks very like Fog Hair, the same Fog Hair that Arthur has. Is this because she has been experimenting with Fog?

3. We found a jar in Marco's garbage can exactly the same as one from the scene of a Fog Attack. Coincidence — or does it have something to do with Fog? (Fog Storage Device?)

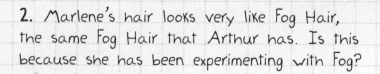

4. Marco claims to be friends with Coco but secretly shouts at photos of her. Why is he lying?

5. Coco fired her hairdresser for being bald. Marco brags about once being Coco's hairdresser and is also BALD!

6. Hair by Marco is on Puddleford Main Street. His salon is near where all the Fog Attacks (Hair Horror Hotspots) have taken place. (But so is Kurl Up and Dye.)

VERDICT: We don't have any concrete evidence (like catching Marco making Fog) so we can't confront him. We need to interview Coco to see if our theory is correct. If she did fire Marco, we should probably warn her that he may be plotting revenge at the concert.

stage

11:00 AM
PUDDLEFORD PARK
(COCO NUTELLO CONCERT ENTRANCE GATE)

Getting to see Coco wasn't as easy as we'd thought.

"We need to speak to Coco," I said to the security guard, who was patrolling the huge fence that has been put up around the park. I tried to sound really confident, like he should just let us in without any messing around.

"Sorry, you can't come in. Gates open tonight at six-thirty," said the guard.

SECURITY

"But this is urgent! There's a bald hairdresser – we think he wants revenge on Coco!" said Violet.

I can't believe Violet said that! That is what we think is going on, but to anyone not involved with the case, it just sounds stupid!

"Listen, I've had Coco's crazy fans here all day trying to get in. Like I told the weird kid with the beehive, gates open at six-thirty." He locked the gates and walked away.

Great. We didn't get to speak to Coco and we've been mistaken for crazed Nutello fans like Arthur. (I doubt there are many other fans with beehives hanging around so the guard must have been talking about him.)

crazed
Nutello
fan

I LOVE Coco!

2:00 PM
OUTSIDE HAIR BY MARCO. HIDING BEHIND
THE GARBAGE CANS. AGAIN.

Since we can't get to Coco, we've decided to keep an eye on Marco in case he tries anything. There have been many shocking haircuts leaving the salon but no Fog Hair. No sign of Marlene – is she up to something Fog-related in the back room?

Marco has just finished cutting a lady's hair. It's another weird one. The lady can't see where she is going as she leaves the salon because of her long bangs.

Can't see

139

Hang on! Marlene is coming into the salon. Her beehive hairstyle is bright orange today. It looks like a traffic cone. Surely she hasn't been silly enough to get caught up in The Fog three times. I am almost certain that *is* Fog Hair.

"If that is what they've got planned for Coco I think her career could be over." said Poppy. "No more hair swishing."

traffic cone hair

traffic cone

(Alien costumes on, eyebrows secured)

5:10 PM
STILL OUTSIDE HAIR BY MARCO

Interesting development! Marco seems to have decided to close the shop early. He's drawn the blinds. Is he getting ready to go to the Coco Nutello concert?

Wait. What's that? Is that Fog? Coming from under the door of the salon?

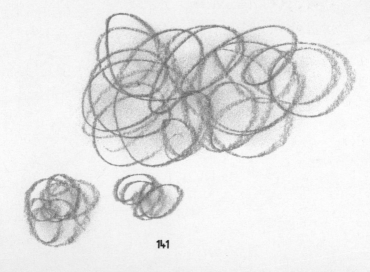

I didn't have time to write this while Operation Hair Scare was in progress, so I've just written up an account of when and how everything happened. Prepare for **total weirdness!**

Violet

Operation
Hair Scare

MYSTERY KIT

POPPY

me →

5:40 PM
HAIR BY MARCO, HAIR WASHING SINKS.

Huge clouds of Fog were pouring out from under the front door of Hair by Marco. There were people passing by on their way to the concert – without hats on. (Had nobody read our Fog Avoidance Advice?)

"Poppy, clear the area. Violet, watch my back. I'm going in," I said.

"Mariella, I don't like this! At least let's put a shower cap on, for added hair security," said Violet.

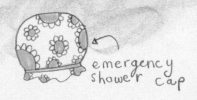

emergency shower cap

"THERE ISN'T TIME!" I screamed,
as I ran from our hiding place to the door of
the salon.

I heard Poppy trying to clear passers-by and Violet
shouting she couldn't find the shower caps. I barged
into the salon – the door wasn't even locked. Either
Marco and Marlene had been taken by surprise, or
they didn't care people were going to know it was
them! All I could see was thick purple Fog. It was
even worse than the Galaxy Gang attack.

**"STOP! IN THE NAME OF THE MYSTERY
GIRLS – STOP!"**
I shouted into the purple haze. (I'd been
practicing my serious voice for ages, but in an
actual dramatic mystery situation it sounded
all wobbly.)

"MWHAAA HA HA HA HA HAAAA!"

A hideous laughter filled the salon and I heard
a door slam.

"Um, hello, is anyone there? **STOP IN THE NAME OF THE MYSTERY GIRLS!**" I said again.

Through the smoke, I heard a sniffling noise. It was coming from behind the sinks.

"Don't come any closer!" said a voice, as a towel flew out at me.

Marlene!

We'd managed to catch a prime suspect and now it was time for some answers.

"You can't get upset just because we've caught you!" said Poppy from the doorway. "You ruined my swim meet – and my eyebrows."

Marlene's sniffles turned into sobs.

three shower caps

"Um, is she OK?" said Violet, coming up behind Poppy. (She'd found the shower caps and was wearing all three.)

I peered behind the sinks. Marlene was trying to conceal her hair using a towel, without much success. There were patches of pink, blue, white, and green, and strange matted parts that looked very much like tentacles coming out of her head.

"It wasn't my fault!" she cried. "Marco made me do it!"

At last! A confession!

"Marlene," I said. "Tell us everything."

tentacle

HIDEOUS

5:55 PM
STAFF ROOM, HAIR BY MARCO

It took a long time to get any sense out of Marlene.
Even though she was crying, none of us felt like
being nice to her.

"It wasn't meant to go
this far!" said Marlene.

It was a little late for that,
I thought. But instead,
I said, "What do you
mean exactly?"

"My hair is stuck like this!" Marlene said, wailing.

"Don't worry – the hairdressers at Kurl Up and
Dye can fix it," said Violet.

"NO! It's permanent! That's what Marco told me before he ran off!" Marlene cried.

Oh no. Marlene's hair is the worst case of **Hair Horror** we've seen yet. What does she mean there's no cure?

"I thought he was trying to create a product that made really cool hairstyles. I just wanted cool hair – not this!" she said.

I decided to get to the point. "Look, does all this have something to do with Coco Nutello firing Marco?"

"Yes! How do you know? I only found out because I overheard him shouting at that picture of her on the wall," she said. "He's bald, you know, that's why she fired him. He wants revenge for being fired. He said it ruined his career!"

coco nutello

I knew it!

"He knew he would never get past Coco's security so he made a Fog Blowing machine from a jar and an old hairdryer – that way he can target her from a distance. He's been practicing with it all week," Marlene continued.

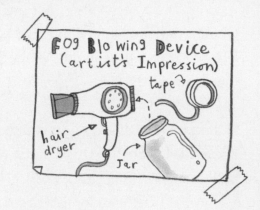

Fog Blowing Device
(artist's Impression)
tape?
hair dryer
Jar

The whirring noise and the jar!

"I kept telling him to stop but he said if I kept quiet he'd make me senior stylist," Marlene sobbed. "He ran off, with a jar full of Fog. You need to stop him, he doesn't care who ends up with Fog Hair, as long as he gets Coco!"

Poppy, Violet, and I all looked at each other in horror. The concert was about to begin – we had to get to Coco before Marco did!

7:05 PM
PUDDLEFORD PARK, CROWD AT COCO NUTELLO CONCERT

When we finally got into the park (there was a really long line – it was really annoying), Coco was on stage. We couldn't see Marco anywhere. Just a sea of sequined bows and sparkly berets. Berets were not going to offer full head protection against The Fog!

Coco really cannot sing live. She sounded awful. She was prancing around dressed as a witch's cat pretending to escape from her backup dancers, who were dressed like zombies.

Zombie dancer

151

She was holding the zombies off by swishing her long hair around wildly. The crowd was going crazy for it. (It seemed a strange thing to do if zombies were after you.)

Then the mega-annoying *I Love Dancin' on Tables* began to play and Coco started doing that stupid dance routine Arthur has been practicing for weeks – jumping around on tables with the wind machines blowing her shiny hair everywhere.

wind machines

Hang on! The wind machines! If Marco unleashed The Fog near them, Coco and all of Puddleford would never have normal hair again.

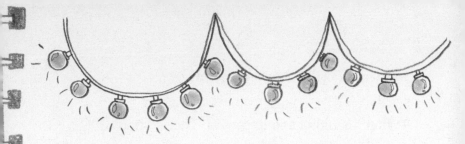

7:40 PM
PUDDLEFORD PARK, NEAR HOT DOG VANS

I scanned the crowd for any sign of Marco.
Nothing. As we got nearer to the stage the
wind machines picked up speed – it looked as
if Coco was in a hurricane, her hair flying
around everywhere.

Hurricane hair!

Suddenly Poppy shouted, **"FOG!"**

At first I couldn't see anything. Then I spotted it. A cloud of Fog a few feet away at the bottom of the steps that led to the stage.

Through the bobbing heads of the crowd I saw The Fog engulf the two security guards who had

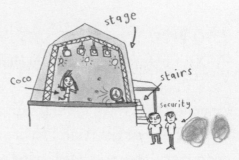

been guarding the entrance. Then Marco leaped out from behind a burger van and ran into the cloud.

"He's trying to get up on stage with her!"
I shouted. "Follow him!"

We pushed our way through the jumping crowds
toward The Fog Cloud.

"Arrrgghhhhhh!" We all screamed as
we ran through The Fog up the steps. (Hair and
eyebrows covered.)

Marco was going to be on the stage any minute.
It would take him a few seconds to release
The Fog, and then the wind machines would
blow it everywhere. After everything that had
happened, were we too late?

APPREHENDING A SUSPECT

In some situations it is up to the mystery solver to apprehend a suspect before the authorities arrive to take over. This can be both a thrilling and daunting experience. Remember to think carefully, stay safe, and to expect the unexpected. Just follow these simple steps:

1. Tracking and Identification

Make sure you have the right person in your sights. You could give an innocent person a nasty fright if you don't.

2. Distraction and Confusion

Catch your suspect off guard by doing something that will temporarily startle them.

Leap from behind a tree

Play a mysterious tune

Burst a balloon

3. Containment

You may wish to:

A: Use a net (available from the Young Super Sleuth's catalog).

B: Push them into a lockable room.

C: Pin the suspect down, sitting on them until help arrives.

4. Clarification

State clearly who you are and what the suspect is accused of doing. They may try to deny their guilt but be firm – this could be your only chance to wrap up the mystery.

TOP TIP

Hair clip voice recorder

Keep a voice recorder on you at all times; you may be able to capture the suspect admitting their guilt on tape!

7:45 PM
COCO NUTELLO GIG, SIDE STAGE ENTRANCE

We ran through another Fog cloud – and there he was. He must have realized he was being followed. (Maybe we shouldn't have been screaming and shouting so much.)

"MWAH, HA HA HA HA HAAAAAA!"

Marco pulled something from his pocket. The Fog Blowing Device! It was just like Marlene had described – a hairdryer attached to a jar filled with swirling Fog. He pointed it at us and released another cloud of Fog.

"That's not going to stop us!" I shouted.
"STOP IN THE NAME OF THE MYSTERY GIRLS!"
(I really like saying that.)

We fought our way through The Fog and onto
the stage.

It all happened really quickly after that. Marco
sprinted past the backup dancers toward Coco
and the wind machines. Coco was still jumping
around on a table, swishing her hair.

"Noooooooo!" I cried. Marco was aiming
his Fog Blowing Device at the wind machines.
I didn't know if I had time to stop him, but I
had to try.

marco

wind machines

coco

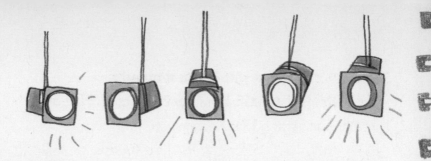

As I ran forward, the music stopped. Coco's band looked confused, as if they weren't sure whether to carry on playing. Coco and her dancers turned to stare at Marco.

But Marco didn't seem worried. He just smiled and looked right at Coco, holding the Fog Blowing Device.

The crowd booed. (I think because the music had stopped, not because they'd guessed they were all about to be Fog Victims.)

"What's that little bald man doing here? I thought I'd fired him," said Coco, looking puzzled.

She wasn't doing herself any favors saying stupid stuff like that. It was definitely not a good thing to say to a man holding Coco's worst bad hair day nightmare – in a jar.

"YOU DID FIRE ME!"

roared Marco. "And I'm here to show you I am not some 'little bald man'!"

"What are you going on about, Baldy?" said Coco, swishing her hair.

Just then, the two security guards Marco
had taken out with The Fog
stumbled on stage, looking
confused. They had
the same hideous
tentacle hair as
Marlene.

"I'm talking about FOG HAIR,
Coco," Marco said, pointing to
the security guards. "You, and
all your fans, are going to have
bad hair days FOREVER! We'll
see how many fans you've got
left after that!"

The audience gasped.

Even Coco looked scared now.

Marco raised the Fog Blowing
Device and aimed it at
the wind machines.
He was still smiling
weirdly.

"You can't do that! I'm the
face of Coco Nutello Hair
Care!" Coco said. "Somebody
do something! HELP!"

She screamed.

It looked as if this was the end of Coco's hair –
and the hair of everyone in Puddleford.

7:55 PM
STILL ON STAGE WITH COCO, AND A TOTALLY INSANE HAIRDRESSER

"MWAH, HA HA HA HA HAAAAAA!"

Marco paused for another dramatic evil laugh.
It was the opportunity I'd been waiting for.
I leaped forward and grabbed the Fog Blowing
Device from his hands.

Marco looked startled. Then Violet threw herself
to the floor and pulled the plug on the wind
machines. (Nice work, Violet.)

me

"What? NOOOOO!"

Marco screamed.

The audience cheered.

"What are you waiting
for?" called Poppy to the
two security guards.
"Get him!"

"Awesome!" said Coco, as
Marco was pinned to the floor.

"No! You can't do this!" cried Marco. "I'll get
you — I'll get you all!"

"Whatever," said Coco.

Then she turned to Poppy, Violet, and me and said,
"Thanks, Nutello Nuts! I'm, like, totally grateful and
stuff. You can be my special backstage guests!"

"All in a day's work for the Mystery Girls," I said, grinning. (I was enjoying the moment too much to say that actually the Mystery Girls aren't Nutello Nuts and that Coco should be more careful who she annoys.)

The audience cheered again and lights flashed and glittery confetti scattered over us.

"What can I say?" I said, as Coco passed me a microphone. "Other than, you don't need to wear hats any more!"

The crowd went crazy, flinging sequined berets into the air. (Which were totally unsuitable head protection anyway, but never mind.) Yessss!

Sunday
November 1st

Puddleford is a **Hair Scare** free zone!

The Mystery Girls and Coco

Fog!

Arthur practicing the Coco Flick

1:30 PM
MYSTERY GIRLS HQ

Even though I'm not a Coco fan, it was pretty cool being her backstage guests. Arthur is completely jealous.

There was this huge sofa and Poppy, Violet, and I just lay on it while people brought us free food. (I would have preferred it if *I Love Dancin' on Tables* hadn't been playing on repeat though.)

cupcake

After the security guards caught Marco, Detective Sparks from Puddleford Police came to take the Fog Blowing Device away. He says it's a key piece of evidence and it's really good that the Mystery Girls managed to get it to them safely.

Marco is being questioned. The police aren't sure what to charge him with yet though. They say they've never seen a case like this one.

I felt sorry for Marlene in the end. She never meant to get so involved, and she was totally distraught about having permanent Fog Hair.

Luckily Kurl Up and Dye have come to the rescue again – they managed to find a shampoo to fade the multi-colored patches, and loosen the tentacles of matted hair.

Shirley said she liked Marlene's style and has offered her a trainee hairdresser's job. Marlene had wanted a senior stylist position but Shirley told her she was pushing her luck.

still in a mood

Marlene's faded Fog Hair

Barbara said the salon is getting really booked up (not just for Fog Hair Victims) now that they are the only hairdressers in Puddleford, so they need an extra pair of hands.

It's been crazy since the Coco gig – the Puddleford Gazette and the Official Coco Nutello Fansite are going to do a special story on the Mystery Girls and how we solved this case. I bet we'll get tons of calls from people who want us to solve mysteries for them.

I've just finished our case report:

CASE REPORT: HUGE HAIR SCARE

SOLVED BY THE MYSTERY GIRLS (HAIR-RELATED MYSTERY EXPERTS)

After being fired from his celebrity hairstylist position by Coco Nutello (for being bald), Marco Hambleton-Jones opened his own salon in Puddleford, where he knew Coco would be coming on her tour. Here he plotted his revenge.

Marco knew he'd never be allowed to style Coco's hair, not after being fired, so the only way to get near enough to mess it up was to create a high strength spray (Fog) that transformed hair into strange styles quickly. And, from a distance, if he couldn't get through security.

At first, Marco's assistant, Marlene, was happy for Marco to experiment on her, because she liked the unusual hairstyles The Fog created. (She thought it was a new styling product.)

spikey   giant beehive   traffic cone

But Marco also used his Fog Hair formula on twenty-five innocent people. He wanted to make the most embarrassing hairstyle ever, which is why we saw lots of different styles on Fog Victims.

← fog victims

Marco invented a strange hairdryer device with a glass jar attached to blow The Fog at victims. This explains the whirring noise heard by some Fog Victim witnesses.

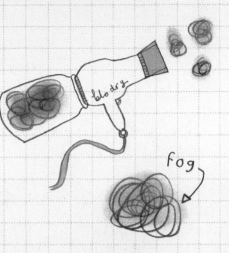

fog

Although the effects of Fog Hair fade over time, the talented stylists at Kurl Up and Dye have found a way of speeding the process up using their special De-Foggifying treatments.

before

extra strong shampoo

after

faded Fog Hair

new hairstyle hat

We would like to officially confirm it is OK to go outside without a hat. (Although Mom's knitted hairstyle hats are now so popular that many people are choosing to wear them, rather than bother to style their actual hair.)

The Mystery Girls are free to take on another mystery — get in touch if anything weird has happened to you. (We are now definitely experts in WEIRD mysteries.)

CASE CLOSED

watson's beehive is fading!

Poppy's fog Brows — almost normal!

me

ACKNOWLEDGMENTS

A huge thank you to my agent, Mark, and everyone at Orion for their tireless enthusiasm for all things Mystery Girl. (Mariella would totally let you all become Mystery Girls, even the boys.)

A special mention to Jenny Glencross – editor extraordinaire – for her support and advice on Mariella's most complicated case yet (so mysterious it baffled me for a while).

I have dedicated this book to my dad and my brother as they have both provided hair related inspiration. My brother's past love of wild hair experimentation and home hair dye kits gave me lots of funny ideas for scary hair.

And I couldn't help being reminded of a childhood story my dad told me. He reportedly had his own Huge Hair Scare in Wavertree Mystery (an aptly named Liverpool park). He claimed his hair "blew away" in a freak gust of wind – resulting in the baldness we see today. A convincing story that I completely believed to be true, until my Mystery Senses tuned in that is …

Kate Pankhurst, 2013

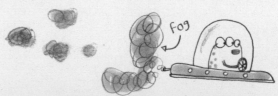

fog